THIS BOOK BELONGS TO

Cat WitH dRaCuLa COStuMe

Little cute GHOSt

PUMPKiN WiTH WiTCH HaT

Halloween demon costume

cute cat inside pumpkin

Little MUMMY BOY

ice cream pumpkin

cute faced GHOSt

GHOSt anGEL of deatH

frankenstein cat

Witch Preparing Portion

Halloween children party

HaLLOWeeN WitcH cOStuMe

Halloween Monster Costume

CELEBRATING HALLOWEEN

dRacULa CatCHiNG Bat

CHILDREN DINOSAUR COSTUMES

PUMPKIN AIR BALLOON

cute Sitting cat

flYinG Bat WitH PuMPKin

dRacuLa and PuMPKinS

Halloween Ghost Costume

Cat With Pumpkin Head

Halloween Pumpkin Costume

FLYING PUMPKIN BOY

Little Monster With Heart Love

flYiNG GHOSt

cute flying Bat

funny pumpkin

funny cat above pumpkin

Made in the USA
Las Vegas, NV
09 October 2022